First published in the United States, Great Britain, Canada, Australia, and New Zealand in 1996
by North-South Books, an imprint of Nord-Süd Verlag AG, Gossau Zürich, Switzerland.

Text copyright © 1992 by Neuer Malik Verlag, Kiel
Illustrations copyright © 1996 by Nord-Süd Verlag AG, Gossau Zürich, Switzerland
This illustrated edition first published in Switzerland under the title *Fatima und der Traumdieb*
English translation copyright © 1996 by North-South Books Inc.
The text for this edition has been adapted by the author.

Distributed in the United States by North-South Books Inc., New York.

Library of Congress Cataloging-in-Publication Data is available.
A CIP catalogue record for this book is available from The British Library.
ISBN 1-55858-653-9 (TRADE BINDING)
1 3 5 7 9 TB 10 8 6 4 2
ISBN 1-55858-654-7 (LIBRARY BINDING)
1 3 5 7 9 LB 10 8 6 4 2
Printed in Germany

For more information about our books, and the authors and artists
who create them, visit our web site: http://www.northsouth.com

Rafik Schami
Fatima and
the Dream Thief

Els Cools 🦋 Oliver Streich

Translated by Anthea Bell

North-South Books
New York · London

ONCE UPON A TIME there was a widow who lived with her two children, Hassan and Fatima. Her husband, a poor woodcutter, had died soon after their daughter's birth. Every day the woman went to the nearby monastery to help with the washing, cooking, and gardening, and every evening she came home worn out, undid her little bundle, and gave Hassan and Fatima what little food she had brought back with her.

One day, when Hassan was fourteen, the widow fell sick from exhaustion.

"Mother," said Hassan, "we have only enough flour and salt, onions and potatoes, to last two weeks. I'm going out to look for work."

"But you're still a child, my son!" said his mother in a feeble voice.

Hassan went off, all the same. He asked every shopkeeper and merchant in the town square, but hard as he tried he found no work all day. When it was growing dark, he saw the lights of a great castle in the distance, and hurried that way.

It was late when Hassan reached the castle gate. He knocked.

A tall man opened the gate. "What do you want?" he asked.

"Do you have any work for me, sir?"

"Indeed I do, but you won't last long. No one lasts longer than a week here."

"Why—is the work so hard?"

"No, the work is child's play, but I don't like a servant to lose his temper. Do you often get angry?"

"Not often, but sometimes."

"Then you won't last long here."

"How much would you pay me?" asked Hassan.

"If you work for me without losing your temper, you'll get one gold coin every week, and I'll pay you on Saturday evening. But if you do lose your temper, you won't get a penny, and I'll take away your dreams—all your wonderful dreams. Your deep and restful sleep will be gone forever. Do you still want to work for me?"

"I never lose my temper," said Hassan cheerfully, going through the gate.

The same evening the master of the castle told Hassan what he had to do.

Every morning he was to light the fire in the hearth, milk the fat cow, and lead the fine horse ten times around the yard. In the afternoon he was to clean the Persian carpet and put soft cushions on it, light the incense in the little silver dish, and serve his master's exotic Gold Peking tea. Hassan did all this every day. He was amazed by the size of the castle. He counted a hundred and one rooms in it, and he was allowed into all but one of them. There were floors made of marble, walls made of silver, and ceilings of gold. Only one room was always kept locked. An old woman came every day in the morning, cleaned the castle until sunset, and then left again. She never said a word, and Hassan did not like the dark looks she gave him. He worked hard and smiled more cheerfully day by day. And night after night he lay in his little room in the attic, dreaming of the moment when he would proudly hand his mother the gold coin.

Early on Saturday morning the boy jumped out of bed. First he went to the kitchen. He lit the fire on the hearth as he did every morning, and went off to the cow shed, whistling. There he milked the cow and came back to the kitchen with the bucket of milk. His master was already waiting for him.

"I wish you a very good morning!" cried Hassan, but the lord of the castle only smiled in a strange way.

"Let me see that!" he barked at his servant, snatching the pail from his hand and looking at it. "You've been drinking some of this milk!" he shouted.

"But sir, I never drink milk."

"You dare to say I'm lying?" roared the lord of the castle.

"Oh no sir, never! I only . . ." But Hassan didn't finish what he was saying, because his master emptied the bucket over his head.

Hassan was quivering with rage, but he clenched his teeth when the lord of the castle asked, "Are you angry?"

"No," replied Hassan, surprised by his master's diabolical laughter.

"Good. Let's hope your good temper lasts. Go and see to the horse."

Hassan went, wiping the milk off his face and seething inside with humiliation.

It was icy cold outside. Hassan's wet clothes were clinging to his skin, and he was trembling. "I mustn't get angry," he muttered. "I just mustn't get angry. . . ." He led the horse ten times around the great yard, as he did every day. His fingers were so cold that they hurt. Then, half frozen, Hassan went into the kitchen to warm his hands by the fire.

"You've finished very quickly today!" thundered his master's voice. "Did you go around the yard ten times?" he asked, and he laughed.

"Yes sir, I went around it ten times."

"Did you go around to the right or the left?" asked his master.

Hassan looked at him in surprise. "To the left . . . no, to the right, the same as usual."

"Heavens above!" cried the man in horror. "So that's why my fine horse is in such a bad way! You must go to the left, so do ten rounds now to make up for the wrong ones, and then ten proper rounds so that my horse will feel better again."

"But sir, it's very cold!"

"A servant doesn't contradict his master, unless he's angry. Are you angry?"

"No, I never get angry," Hassan mumbled, rushing out. He led the horse twenty times around the yard to the left, whispering to himself all the time: "I just mustn't get angry. It will soon be over."

When he brought the horse back to the stable, he felt exhausted. There sat the silent cleaning woman as if she had been waiting for him. She looked at him with concern, went over to him, pressed his hands, and smiled as if to encourage him. But Hassan pushed her away. "You're bringing me bad luck today! Leave me alone!" he cried, hurrying into the castle.

His master had just finished eating. "Now get my carpet and cushions ready for me!" he said.

Slowly Hassan went into the big room where every day he brushed the Persian carpet and shook up the cushions, so that the lord of the castle could

enjoy his tea in the pleasant scent of incense. But when Hassan had brushed the carpet, which was clean anyway, the lord of the castle trampled all over it with his dirty boots. Then he went out again. The carpet was filthy now, and Hassan had to begin all over again. Just as he was finishing, however, the lord of the castle came back into the room and made the carpet dirty again.

"Oh, sir!" groaned Hassan.

"What is it?" laughed the man. "Are you angry to see me back? Just say so, and I won't come back again."

"No, I'm not a bit angry," said Hassan, gritting his teeth, and he went on scrubbing. It was late in the afternoon before the lord of the castle took his dirty boots off. He clapped Hassan on his weary shoulders and shouted, "Now I want my tea!"

Hassan dragged himself into the kitchen to make the Gold Peking tea.

Hassan made the tea, put the pot and a warmed cup on a silver tray, and took it in to the lord of the castle. The Gold Peking tea smelled delicious, but when the man had taken the first sip, he spat it out and pushed the cup away.

"What sort of tea is this?" he shouted. "Did you drink the first brew yourself, and bring me the weak second one?"

"Oh, sir, by my father's soul, I never drank a drop of it!" stammered Hassan in terror.

"Liar! Are you trying to torment me?" shouted the lord of the castle, throwing the teapot at Hassan. It hit him full in the face and fell to the floor.

At this insult Hassan's patience gave way. "That's enough!" he shouted, kicking the teapot against the wall. "What's the idea? Yes, I am angry with you and your mean tricks. I could strangle you! Who do you think you are, eh?"

Hassan shouted as he had never shouted before, but that only seemed to amuse the lord of the castle. He rolled about on his soft cushions shaking with laughter, and then Hassan realized that he had lost. He picked up his coat and left.

The voice of the lord of the castle echoed after him. "Oh, how I'll relish your dreams . . . how I'll *relish* your dreams!"

Hassan was crying as he slammed the castle gate behind him. The old woman was sitting on a flat rock outside the gate. She buried her head in her hands and wept.

With the last of his strength, Hassan ran home, but he didn't get there until midnight. He hesitated outside the door for a long time, for he was ashamed to go in empty-handed. He heard his mother and Fatima talking inside. At last he plucked up his courage and went in.

His mother and sister were overjoyed to see him, but Hassan only wept, and told them about his misfortune. "If I'd been a little cleverer, I could have kept from getting angry for a few more hours. I'm stupid."

"No, brother, you're not stupid," said Fatima. "Wait here with Mother. I'll try my luck and bring you back your dreams."

"Oh, daughter, you're only twelve, and so small and weak!" wailed their mother. But Fatima set off the next morning. She knew there was still enough food at home for another week. Hassan had told her the way to the castle, and so Fatima reached it early in the afternoon. She knocked at the gate and waited.

The gate opened. The silent woman was sweeping the yard. She looked up for a moment, shook her head, and went on working.

"Well, well, what have we here?" cried the lord of the castle. "A little girl! Have you lost your way, or are you begging for a crust of bread?"

"I had a dream yesterday, and it led me to your castle," replied Fatima. "I followed it and now I'm here."

"A dream! And it led you to me?"

"Yes sir. It told me that if I worked here for a week I'd go home rich and happy."

"You can work for me, but you won't last long, because if you get angry you'll lose both your wages and your dreams."

"And what will you pay me for the week?"

"One gold coin," said the lord of the castle.

"Show me, so I know what I'm getting," said Fatima.

The lord of the castle was amazed by her boldness, but he took a shining gold coin from his coat pocket and handed it to Fatima. She took the coin, threw it on the ground several times and listened to the ring of it, then examined it suspiciously and bit its edge.

"It's real," she said.

"But you mustn't lose your temper, for if you do you'll get nothing at all, and you'll lose your dreams into the bargain," repeated the lord of the castle, letting her in.

"I never lose my temper," replied Fatima, entering the yard. "But suppose *you* get angry?"

"I? No one on earth can make me angry!" cried the lord of the castle, amused.

"Still, suppose you do get angry after all?" laughed Fatima.

"Then I'll give you two gold coins," said the lord of the castle, and he showed Fatima what she had to do.

The next day Fatima set to work. She sang and laughed and kept close watch on the lord of the castle, who visited the locked room just before his midday meal. He spent a little while in there and came out very cheerful. Suddenly, as if by magic, the table was piled high with the finest of foods, and with fruit and wines. The lord of the castle ate greedily, chanting, "Oh, how I relish feeding on these dreams!"

Fatima tried with all her might to open the door of the mysterious locked room, but she couldn't do it. Worn out, she lay down on the straw mattress in her room very late at night and fell asleep at once. The next morning she greeted the old woman and smiled at her, and later that day Fatima went up to her, stroked her scarred hands, and smiled at her again, but the woman looked away.

"Did he steal your dreams?" asked Fatima.

The woman turned to the girl, her eyes full of tears, and nodded.

"And did he steal your words, too?"

The old woman nodded again.

Fatima hugged her. "Don't worry, we'll find a way out of this," she promised the woman.

Late that evening Fatima waited until the lord of the castle went to take a bath. She followed him. When she heard him singing in the big bathtub, she went into his dressing room. There lay his silken clothes, and the golden chain with the little key to the locked room. Fatima took a lump of wax out of her pocket and made an impression of the key. The blood froze in her veins when the lord of the castle called: "I hear you out there! I see it all. Don't move!"

But Fatima ran off and climbed into bed. A little later she heard her master opening the door to her room. He held up an oil lamp. "No, she's asleep!" he whispered, and went away.

The next morning she pressed the lump of wax into the old woman's hand, and the old woman hurried to town with it. On Friday she came back and gave Fatima a little brass key. Fatima waited until the lord of the castle had gone to sleep. Then she took the key and stole to the locked room, barefoot. Her heart was thudding as she fitted the key into the lock. She turned it, and lo and behold, the door opened.

A bright light
shone on Fatima as she
entered the room. She stood there,
rooted to the spot. Thousands of little cages
hung in the big room, which had no windows,
and there was a butterfly fluttering helplessly
in each cage. Their wings shimmered and
gleamed like thousands and thousands of stars.
The little girl could hardly tear herself away
from the beauty of the butterflies, but in
the end she hurried out of the room
again and shut the door.

On Saturday morning the lord of the castle smiled at Fatima. "If you last through today, you'll be richer by one gold coin!" he cried, and he smiled slyly.

"I dreamed of being richer by two gold coins," replied Fatima.

"Huh! You'd better see that you get the milk before it turns to yogurt in my valuable cow's udder!" her master warned her.

Fatima took the bucket and went off to the cow shed, whistling. "What are you doing here, poor cow?" she asked. "Eating and sleeping, just to be milked! And he'll slaughter you when your milk dries up. Off with you into the forest! Life may be dangerous there, but it's worth living." With these words she opened the door, gave the cow a hearty slap on the rump with the flat of her hand, and went back into the house with the empty can. As if the cow had understood, she ran off into the forest and was soon lost in the thickets.

"What's this? Haven't you milked my cow yet?" roared the lord of the castle when he saw Fatima with the empty can.

"The cow wouldn't let me. I was going to milk her when she said, 'Go and tell that fat person on two legs I don't want to be milked anymore. I'm off.' That's what she said!"

"You mean my valuable cow has run away?" cried the man.

"Are you angry?" asked Fatima, smiling.

The lord of the castle saw his mistake at once. He smiled. "No, but I don't believe you. Go and saddle my horse. I'm going to ride after the cow and ask her if she told you that, and if you lied, then you must clean out the stable and the yard too with a toothbrush, and without getting angry, either. Hurry up! I've no time to waste."

Fatima hurried to the stable. She took off the horse's bridle and said, "Oh, horse, see how fine you look without a bridle. Out there are the mountains and rivers where you long to gallop. Why stay in this stinking stable? Off you go!" And with these words she slapped him on the rump, and the horse raced away like an arrow.

"The horse didn't want to carry you any longer," said Fatima when she came back to her master. "He says you were much too heavy for his back, and he'd rather go out and see the world."

"This is too much! My fine horse gone! I can't have understood you correctly!" cried the lord of the castle.

"Oh yes you did. But I see you're angry!" laughed Fatima.

"No, I'm not!" he shouted. "Cows and horses can be bought, and I can never be angry about something money can buy. Now go and make my tea."

"What, now?"

"Yes, now!"

"But I haven't had my breakfast yet," said Fatima, taking a loaf from the bread basket.

"I forgot to tell you," the lord of the castle said. "My servants aren't allowed to eat on Saturday. Put that bread down and go and make my tea, quick!"

"I get so forgetful and hard of hearing when I don't eat. What was it you just said?"

"Make my Gold Peking tea!" bellowed the lord of the castle.

"How funny! You really want to drink that?" asked Fatima.

"What's so funny about it? I drink it every day!" he shouted.

"Are you sure?"

"Yes!" he groaned.

Fatima busied herself at the hearth for a while, and came back with a large, steaming teapot. Her master took one sip and started coughing and spluttering.

"What's this, then?" he shouted, wiping his mouth in disgust.

"Old-stocking tea," replied Fatima.

"*What* did you make it with?"

"Old stockings. I was surprised myself. I thought I must be wrong. But you said yes, that's what you wanted to drink."

"I said Gold Pcking, not old stocking!" growlcd thc lord of thc castlc.

"I'm so sorry. My empty stomach does make me rather hard of hearing. Are you angry now?" asked Fatima.

"No!" said her master, smiling grimly.

"Oh yes you are," Fatima replied, and she hurried out.

The old woman beamed at her.

"Only a few more hours and then you'll have your dreams back," whispered Fatima as she helped the woman with her work. Just before midday she stopped and looked at the old woman. "Now's the time," she said.

The woman dropped the broom and hurried into the castle with Fatima. Fatima opened the door to the butterflies' prison and set them all free from their cages. They fluttered out of the room and flew out of the castle in a cloud of different hues. Two butterflies settled on the old woman's head and mouth and kissed her. Then the woman laughed and said, "My name is Miriam." Fatima and Miriam fell into each other's arms, and when they had helped the last butterfly out into the light of day, they closed the door quietly and left.

It wasn't long before they heard the lord of the castle bellowing, "Where are the dreams? Who stole them? Where are the dreams? They are food and drink to me! How am I ever to eat now?"

"You would do well to starve, you nasty fat pig!" hissed Miriam.

Fatima doubled up with laughter when the lord of the castle suddenly appeared in the doorway, staring at Miriam. "You . . . you c-c-can . . . sp-speak again?"

"Are you deaf, you donkey?" replied Fatima, shaking with happy laughter.

"So you stole the butterflies!" said her master, his throat dry.

"And you're angry, aren't you? Admit it!" cried Fatima.

"Oh yes, that made me angry, but you're a thief, so you won't get a penny!" said the lord of the castle furiously.

Fatima reached for a stout stick, and Miriam picked up her broom. "We'll see about that," they said, and they beat the man until he begged for mercy and gave them each ten gold pieces.

Miriam hugged Fatima, kissed her, and danced around and around with her, and then she hurried off. "Good-bye, brave girl!" she kept calling, until she disappeared over the hill.

Fatima was going straight through the forest when she heard the horse whinnying. He came trotting towards her. Fatima jumped on his back and rode away. It was dark when she reached her home, but she was delighted to find her mother better and her brother very happy. He hadn't been able to sleep for days, but today a butterfly with bright wings had come fluttering in and kissed him on the forehead before flying back up into the blue sky. Hassan had immediately fallen into a deep sleep, and dreamed of Fatima.

Their mother brewed the fine Gold Peking tea Fatima had brought home with her, and the three of them sat up until far into the night celebrating the happy ending to the story I've just told you.